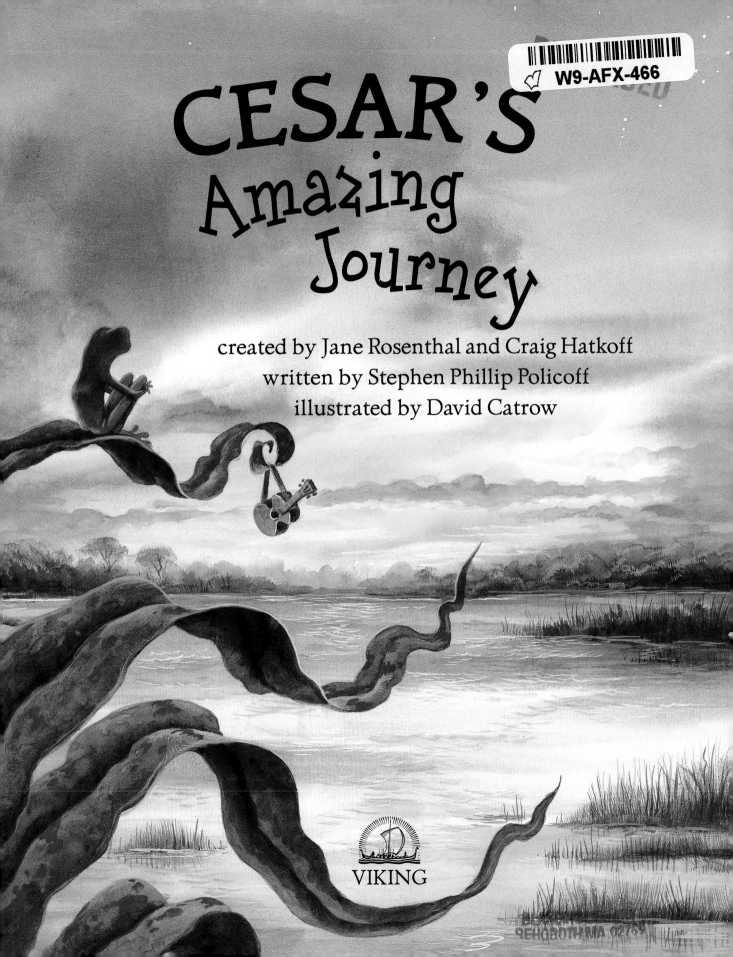

CESAR'S
Amazing
Journey

created by Jane Rosenthal and Craig Hatkoff
written by Stephen Phillip Policoff
illustrated by David Catrow

VIKING

Cesar loved summer nights at home in the Florida wetlands.
Curled up on his banana leaf, he listened to the grown-up tree
frogs fill the warm night with their song.
Sometimes, he even sang, too:

TOWHEE! TOWHEE!
HAPPY TO BE
SAFE AND SNUG
IN MY OWN LITTLE TREE!

But one morn-
ing, Cesar felt a
bump and a thump.
The whole tree was
shaking! Cesar clung
to his leaf with his toepads as
the tree was lifted up up up
then tossed down down down
into a truck. *Slam!* went the
door.

It was so dark! It was so quiet! At first,
Cesar could only hear the sound of the truck
rumbling up the road. After a while, he heard a tiny
voice from another tree.

Cesar peeked over the top of his leaf. He saw a spider wearing
sunglasses and a straw hat. He was reading a tiny map and singing
to himself.

"Hi, I'm Cesar. Did the humans take your tree, too?"

"No way!" said the spider. "I'm hitching a ride. We are headed for
the most amazing city on earth—New York!"

"New York!" Cesar said. "I don't know anything about New York!"

"It's big! It's fast! We'll have a blast. I'm a traveling spider; the
name's B. Cider."

"That's a funny name," said Cesar.

"Don't you know the nursery rhyme? *Along came a spider and sat down ... B. Cider!*" He lifted four legs above his head. "Tah-dah!" He smiled but Cesar didn't smile back. "Hey, ace, why the long face?"

"I don't get it, Mr. Cider. Why would the humans take my tree to New York?"

B. Cider shrugged. "Humans are crazy! First they cut down the trees, see? Then they build tall buildings. Then they put trees inside the offices because they miss nature! See? Crazy!"

"I've never been to a city," Cesar said, sniffling a little. "I'm cold and scared and I miss my warm wetlands."

B. Cider took off his sunglasses. "You do look kind of shaky and gray, amigo," he said.

And with that, Cesar's tears plopped down on the banana leaf.

B. Cider hopped onto the leaf and put one leg around Cesar's shoulder. "We'll find you a safe spot again, pal. It'll be okay!"

Inside the dark truck, Cesar and B. Cider didn't know how much time had gone by before the truck door swung open.

"We're in the Big Town!" said B. Cider.

Cesar poked his head out of the truck. He heard loud cars and trucks and sirens wailing. And it was cold. He sat shivering on his leaf, until a human lifted his once-safe tree and carried it toward a big brown building.

Then he hopped down down down, landing in a puddle on the street. B. Cider laughed.

"You tree frogs are slow! Come on, let's go! We'll see the sights, take in a show."

Cesar still felt scared, but there was so much to see. People dashing in all directions. A little girl walking a huge dog. A boy with green hair whirrrring by on his skateboard.

"Wow!" Cesar said. "This place is wild!"

"We have left the mud of the wetlands
behind!" B. Cider said. "Sitting pretty in the world's
greatest city!"

But Cesar wasn't sure. "It might be great for humans, but I'll miss
all the other frogs."

"Frogs? You want frogs?" B. Cider asked. "I know where there's a
whole roomful! Come on, Cesar. We're going to FAO Schwarz!"

At the nearest subway stop, they skittered down down down the
long stairs just as a train pulled into the station.

On the crowded train they hopped into the pocket of a boy's
baggy jeans. He was going to FAO Schwarz, too.

THE WORLD'S BIGGEST TOY STORE, read the sign above the door. Inside, Cesar saw a big, funny clock with clowns peeking out and dancing teddy bears and singing mice. A giant toy train *klackeda klacked* around and around the store.

"This is amazing!" Cesar said. "You're sure a lot of frogs live here?"

"What am I, new? Of course they do!" B. Cider said. "Look over there, you'll see it's true!"

Cesar almost felt like singing! One whole side of the store was called Frog World. There were more frogs on one shelf than Cesar had ever seen.

"Now, up there—those are some serious frogs!" B. Cider said.

Cesar looked up and saw lots of tree frogs. One frog was riding a tiny bicycle across a high wire. Two others were doing daredevil leaps from a trapeze.

"Hip! Hop! Hooray!" they sang.

"The Paracroakers! Terrific, or what?"

Cesar sighed. "Sure, but they aren't real frogs. They're toy frogs."

"Oh," B. Cider said.

"Okay, okay," B. Cider said, as they headed
back out to Fifth Avenue. "So I made a little
mistake. You hungry, Cesar?" B. Cider went on.
"Food will make you feel more at home. New
York has the best. And I know a great bistro
near Times Square. Follow me and we're there!"

A young woman whizzed by on a bicycle
carrying big envelopes and packages. They
hopped onto her shoulder and *zwoooshed*
through traffic.

"Wheeeee!" shouted Cesar.

When they hopped off again, they were in
the middle of Times Square. There were bill-
boards with giant faces of men, women, even
dogs. A bright neon sign ran around and
around a building, spelling out words like
NEWS and WEATHER and NOW.

In the restaurant, they sat at a small, round table. B. Cider ordered a big steak and began to carve it up with four of his six legs. Cesar just nibbled on some roses in a vase.

The chef seemed very happy to see them. He kept popping out of the kitchen to make sure they were still there.

"You have the most excellent legs, little froggy," he said. "With legs like yours I could prepare such a meal!"

Cesar looked up and saw a big, shiny knife in the chef's hand.

"Uh-oh!" Cesar said. He hopped away just in time. *Whisssshhh! Thunnnnk!* went the knife, landing right next to B. Cider.

"Hey!" B. Cider said. "I'm not finished!"

But the chef chased them around the table.

"Hop on!" Cesar shouted.

B. Cider scrambled onto his buddy's back, and with one big leap they were out the door.

WELL

They found themselves in the alley behind the restaurant. The two friends sat on a garbage bag to catch their breath.

"New York sure is exciting," Cesar said. "But I'm not sure it will ever really feel like home."

"Lots of places can feel like home if you let them," a small voice said. It was coming from a yellow plastic pail.

B. Cider skittered over and knocked on the pail. "Anybody there?" he said.

A snail poked his head out. "S. Cargo is the name," he said. "Chef wanted to serve me for supper, too. Slipped out of my shell. Just rolled along, sad sad sad. One day, a little boy threw this pail in the garbage. Rolled in—presto! Home!"

B. Cider clapped wildly. "See, Cesar? He found his spot—you can too!"

"Just got to keep rolling," S. Cargo said.

B. Cider spun his web on a streetlight and climbed up. "Where shall we roll to next, Cesar?" he asked. "*This* way is my favorite Broadway show—humans dress up like animals. Or we could go *that* way to the dinosaur museum. . . ."

"This has been one of the most amazing days I've ever had," Cesar said. "But I haven't felt warm since we left home. I miss my leaf."

B. Cider rubbed his chin. "I'll find you that leaf, Cesar, without fail!"

The friends headed back to Times Square. A bus packed with tourists swung by. It looked like two buses, one on top of the other. When B. Cider said "Now!" they hopped on the bus, heading west.

When the bus reached the Hudson River, B. Cider led
Cesar onto a long white boat called *The Circle Line*.
B. Cider and Cesar climbed up onto the railing to
watch the sunset as the boat glided down the river.
As soon as B. Cider spotted the big brown building, he
climbed onto Cesar's back.
"No time to stop. Let's hop
hop hop!" he said.
Kaboinnng! Cesar leaped
toward the shore, landing on
the sidewalk right where their
New York adventure had begun.

B. Cider quickly spun a web and scrambled up the big building. He peeked in all the windows. On the seventh floor, he saw the banana trees, standing in round pots.

"End of the race—this is the place!" he said.

Cesar leaped to the seventh floor and slipped through a crack in the window, tumbling down right onto his favorite leaf.

"What was that?" a little girl said. Her name was Amanda. She was waiting for her mom and she was bored bored bored. Amanda peeked into the banana tree. "Cool," she said, "a tiny frog."

She picked Cesar up and held him in the palm of her hand. "You are so cute!" she said.

But Cesar did not feel cute. He felt cold and scared.

"But you're shivering, poor little guy, and you're all gray. Maybe you're sick." She ran across the office. "Mom! Look!"

Suddenly, there was a circle of humans staring down at Cesar. B. Cider crawled down the office wall. "Do not fear! B. Cider's still here!" he said.

"Mom," Amanda said, "this frog needs a doctor!"

Everyone began to scurry around, talking on telephones. Cesar closed his eyes. He didn't want to cry in front of all these people.

"Come on, honey,"
Amanda's mom said.
"We're going to the zoo."
Amanda scooped Cesar into
a paper cup, and they headed for
a long shiny car. "Not so fast!" B. Cider
said, leaping onto Amanda's backpack.
Cesar saw B. Cider grinning at him.
"Now where are we?" he shivered.
"In a limousine! This is quite a scene!
You're a star, Cesar. Know what I mean?"
"Mom, do you hear something funny?"
Amanda asked. But her mom was busy talking on the phone,
and just smiled.

Inside the zoo, humans wearing white coats and rubber gloves picked Cesar up and turned him over.

"He's a little Cuban tree frog," one human said, finally.

"He's scared and cold. That's why he's so gray," added another.

"Hey guys!" B. Cider snorted. "That's not news to me. Can you help my pal here? That's what I want to see!"

The three humans turned to each other. "Let's put him in the rain forest exhibit!"

They carried Cesar into a warm building, where there were trees, and the *kareee! kareee!* of birds, and a sweet-smelling mist, just like at his home in the wetlands.

"I don't feel cold anymore!" Cesar said.

B. Cider watched as they brushed aside ferns and branches, then gently placed Cesar on a big leaf. And as soon as Cesar's toepads touched the leaf, he turned bright green.

Cesar climbed up up up into his new, safe tree. He heard a tap on the window of the exhibit. It was Amanda. She was smiling and waving.

B. Cider was on her shoulder, waving and singing, "Our journey's not done. This is just round one! I'll be back real soon, then we'll have some more fun!"

As Cesar was getting snug on his leaf, another little frog peeked down at him.

"Hi!" she said. "I'm Ann Phoebe Ann. Are you from down south?"

"I've had the most amazing journey," Cesar said. "I saw so much! It was fun to go exploring, but it's great to feel warm and snug again."

"Would you like to sing with me?" asked Ann Phoebe Ann.

Cesar did feel like singing, so Cesar and Ann Phoebe Ann sat in the warm mist of the rain forest exhibit and sang:

TOWHEE! TOWHEE!
HAPPY TO BE
SAFE AND SNUG
IN MY OWN LITTLE TREE!

And unless they are out exploring with B. Cider, you can probably see them singing there right now.